Stories to Grow By

No Room
for Neighbors

A Tale in Which Two Strangers Become Friends

by Kathryn Wheeler
Illustrated by Darcy Bell-Myers

In Celebration™, Grand Rapids, MI

Credits

Author: Kathryn Wheeler
Cover and Inside Illustrations: Darcy Bell-Myers
Project Director/Editor: Alyson Kieda

ISBN: 1-56822-594-6
No Room for Neighbors
Copyright © 1999 by In Celebration™
Ideal • Instructional Fair Publishing Group
a division of Tribune Education
2400 Turner Avenue NW
Grand Rapids, Michigan 49544

Printed in Singapore

Note to Parents

Matthew 22:39—*"Love your neighbor as yourself."*

In this verse, Jesus calls us to love and help our neighbors. This important Christian value is at the heart of the children's story presented here.

Before reading the story: Read the verse. Ask your children to keep the verse in mind as you read the story out loud. Discuss what it means to "love your neighbor as yourself." Have the children look for ways in which the main characters showed love for a neighbor.

After reading the story: Discuss how Billy showed love for his neighbor, Bradley. What happened as a result? Brainstorm ways to show love for neighbors. Did the children learn any other lessons from the story? about worrying? about the advantages of having a neighbor? Encourage the children to do a neighborly deed today.

Bradley Bandicoot lived all by himself, and that's how he liked it. Every night, he went into the desert to look for food. Every morning, he came home to his burrow to sleep. Bradley had 30 guest rooms in his burrow, but he never had guests. Since he had no one to talk to, he talked to himself.

"What a beautiful night!" said Bradley one evening. "Just the night for beetle hunting." Bradley loved beetles more than anything, but they were hard to catch. Usually, he settled for worms or spiders or sometimes even berries.

6

Bradley headed out, his long nose quivering at the thought of beetle pie. Then he saw something odd. He stopped. He stared. He stood up on his hind legs. "That can't be an anthill!" he said to himself. "It's too big. It looks like . . . it almost looks like . . ." Just then, a clod of dirt flew into the air and hit the top of the hill. "It is!" cried Bradley. "Someone *else* is digging a burrow!" His whiskers dancing nervously, Bradley ran away.

7

That night, Bradley caught three fat, black beetles. Instead of being happy, all he could do was worry about his new neighbor. "This is terrible," he said, emptying his beetle-bag on the kitchen table. "What if I hear him snoring all day long? Neighbors are noisy!"

As he rolled out the dough for beetle pie, he said, "What if he blocks off the little creek with all that digging? I won't have any water. And I know he won't want me to come on his land to get water."

Bradley finished baking and went to bed, but he couldn't sleep. He spent the whole day tossing and turning in one guest room after another, worrying about the neighbor. "What if he digs up all the worms and leaves none for me?" he moaned in guest room number 5.

9

Staring at the ceiling in guest room number 27, Bradley whimpered, "Suppose he scares away all the ants? No more candied ants on holidays!"

Just as Bradley finally dozed off in guest room number 11, he had the worst thought of all. Sitting straight up in bed, he cried, "What if he catches all *my* beetles? Oh, no . . . this is terrible!"

10

The next evening, Bradley scurried out early. He wanted to go beetle hunting before the neighbor beat him to it. "I must, I must, I *must* find the beetles first!" Bradley squeaked. After an hour of hunting, he dug up a gleaming beetle. Before Bradley could put his paws around it, the beetle darted up the branch of a thorn bush.

Bradley climbed
up after the beetle.
"Ouch!" he
cried as thorns
caught hold of
his jacket.
"Drat!" he
exclaimed as thorns dug into
his pants. He twisted one way, then
another. He wriggled up and down. It was no good. The
thorns pinned him in place.
"Help, help, HELP!!!!" the little bandicoot cried.

Back in the new burrow, Billy Bilby stopped digging. His tall ears twitched. He stood very still, listening. "Someone is in trouble," he said, dusting off his paws.

Billy loped into the darkness toward the cries for help. When he saw the little bandicoot hanging in the thorn bush, Billy stood up and pulled out the thorns one by one. Then he set Bradley carefully on the ground.

Dizzy from all his twisting, Bradley gasped, "Thank you."
"Don't mention it," said Billy politely. "What are neighbors for?"
"I don't know," said Bradley. "I've never had a neighbor."
The bilby smiled. "Neighbors are for helping
each other," he answered. Then true to his
word, Billy helped the dizzy bandicoot to the
front door of his burrow.

Bradley thought about the bilby's words. What if he'd had a neighbor to help him when the ceiling had caved in on guest room number 29? he wondered. Or that time he fell into the creek and got stuck in the mud climbing out? Maybe having a neighbor wasn't so bad after all.

15

Standing by the door, Bradley had a thought, and gulped. It was so hard to share, but he bravely asked Billy, "Would you like to come in for some beetle pie?"

"That's neighborly of you," said Billy, "but I'm afraid that I don't like beetle pie very much. Too crunchy."

"Really?" Bradley was overjoyed. "How about some worm stew?"

The bilby coughed. "Kind of you, but . . . too squishy."

"Spider muffins?"

The bilby smiled. "Why, thank you! I love spider muffins."

17

The two neighbors became good friends. They helped each other dig new guest rooms. They baked each other spider muffins. They gave each other candied ants on holidays.

In fact, Bradley grew to like Billy so much that he would have shared a beetle pie with him gladly . . . but Billy never did learn to like beetles, even if they were shelled first.

A Note about Bandicoots and Bilbies

Bandicoots are small mammals. Most weigh less than two pounds (0.9 kilograms). They resemble mice with their rounded ears, black eyes, and long tails but, unlike mice, they have very long, narrow, whiskered snouts. Their coarse fur is chiefly golden brown or gray.

Bandicoots are shy, nocturnal animals. They come out at night to eat insects, spiders, and worms.

Most types of bandicoots live in forests and other heavy plant growth areas. Bandicoots dig huge burrows that they usually do not share. Some bandicoots build nests on the ground out of sticks and leaves.

Bandicoots are marsupials and carry their young in pouches. Bandicoots can be found in Australia and New Guinea.

Bilbies are also marsupials. They are larger than bandicoots and are easily recognized by their long, rabbitlike ears. Bilbies have long, striped tails and gray, silky fur. Their ears are without fur and swivel while listening to distant noises. Like bandicoots, bilbies have long noses.

Bilbies are powerful diggers. They dig large burrows with their long, strong back legs.

Bilbies are nocturnal and feed at night on insects, insect larvae, seeds, bulbs, fruit, and fungi.

The bilby is now limited to desert areas of Australia and Queensland.